Twelfth Night

Written by
Celia Rees

Illustrated by
Kisoo Chai

Collins

Cast of characters

Viola/Cesario

Sebastian

Duke Orsino

Lady Olivia

Sir Toby

Sir Andrew

Malvolio

Maria

Feste

Antonio

Chapter 1

"Viola, wake up! The ship's sinking!"

"Sebastian?" Viola could just see her twin brother's shape in the dark cabin. "Sinking?" She grabbed his outstretched hand, and ran along the narrow corridor and up the wooden stairs to the top deck.

The sky was as black as night. Lightning zigzagged down towards the ship where Viola and Sebastian struggled to stay upright. The ship was being tossed like a cork on the inky, boiling sea and was being driven by huge waves nearer and nearer to shore.

"Whatever happens," Sebastian shouted to his sister over the howling wind, "you must swim. Swim for the shore!"

At that moment, with an almighty CRACK, the mast crashed on to the deck. Viola's hold on Sebastian's hand broke and he disappeared off the side of the ship. Sobbing, Viola desperately clung to what was left of the deck.

At that moment, the ship hit the jagged rocks and Viola was thrown into the foaming water.

"Miss? Wake up!"

"Sebastian? I just had a horrible dream." Viola opened her eyes. But it wasn't Sebastian who was talking to her and she wasn't in her cabin. She was on a beach, and as the cold hit her Viola remembered what had happened.

"The ship?" she whispered.

"Sunk, Miss," said the captain. "That was a mighty storm. We didn't have a chance."

"Where's my brother?" Viola scanned the beach for other survivors.

"I saw him swimming strongly. He might still be alive." But the captain's face was enough to tell Viola that Sebastian had drowned.

Viola bit back a sob and looked up at the steep, white cliffs above them. What was she going to do now?

"Where are we?" she asked the captain.

"This is Illyria, Miss. Ruled by Duke Orsino," the captain told her. "They say he's in love with the fair Lady Olivia, daughter of a count. But the lady's father and brother died one after another and now she's so sad that she's shut herself away."

"Perhaps I can serve this lady," Viola thought aloud. "She's lost a brother, like me. We share the same sadness. She might let me stay with her until I think of what to do."

"Oh, no." The captain shook his head. "She won't see anyone, not even the duke, and she sends all his servants away."

"In that case …" Viola thought again. "I'll serve him instead."

The captain shook his head again. "He only employs men."

"I'll disguise myself as a boy, then, and call myself Cesario."

The idea made Viola feel better. Serving the duke might help take her mind off the death of her brother and would give her time to think about what to do next.

Chapter 2

"I don't know why she's making this fuss," Lady Olivia's uncle, Sir Toby, grumbled. "This endless mourning for her brother. I get told off for having any fun at all."

They were out in the garden. Sir Toby was sitting on a bench enjoying the sunshine, watching Maria, Lady Olivia's maid, sweeping up after the recent storm.

"You shouldn't be late in every night," Maria said, "disturbing everybody, bringing back fools like that Sir Andrew. He'd the cheek to ask my lady to marry him. The very idea!"

"Sir Andrew's a good man!"

9

"He's an idiot!"

"A *rich* idiot."

"You keep him here to spend his money. Move your feet!" Maria hit his boots with her broom. "Here he comes now."

"Sir Andrew! We were just talking about you!"

"Your niece won't have me, Sir Toby." Sir Andrew threw himself down on the bench.

Maria leant on her broom. As if her lady would even *look* at him. He was tall and skinny with his hose all wrinkled round his knees, and that hair! There was more curl in a piece of string.

Sir Andrew shook his head. "I'm going home."

"You can't do that!" Sir Toby gave him a reassuring pat. "You mustn't give up. She won't see the duke, either. You stand as much chance as he does."

"You're right." Sir Andrew straightened up. "I stand as much chance as he does. I'll stay another month."

11

Chapter 3

Duke Orsino was restless, yet he couldn't settle to anything. Lady Olivia still wouldn't see him and sent back every messenger. It'd been weeks now.

"Where's that new boy, Cesario?"

"Here, my Lord."

Viola hurried to his side. With her hair cut short and her boy's clothes, she looked just like the other young men at Orsino's court.

"Cesario!" The duke gave a rare smile. Orsino liked this new lad. He might have more luck with Lady Olivia than the others. He put his arm round the boy's shoulders. "I want you to do something for me."

"Anything, my Lord," Viola replied, her voice as deep as she could manage.

"Go to Lady Olivia." The duke pulled her closer. "Make sure you get in to see her. Don't let anyone stop you."

"If I do get to speak to her, what shall I say?"

"Tell her how much I love her, of course! She might listen to you. Someone young, someone less … threatening." He looked down at Viola. "Why, with that smooth skin," he touched her face, "you could almost be a girl …"

"I'll do my best, Sir." Viola felt herself blushing so she made her voice gruffer.

"I knew I could rely on you!" Orsino smiled. "Perhaps I'll go hunting this morning!"

Viola bowed. She didn't want to let the duke down, but she was going to find the task he'd set her very difficult. He was simply the finest man she'd ever met. Charming, handsome, tall and strong, yet kindly and gentle. From almost the first moment she saw him, she'd been in love with him, but he thought that she was a boy and he was in love with someone else. What was she going to do? Here she was being sent off to this lady, when it was Viola herself who wanted to be his wife.

Chapter 4

"Where've you been, Feste?" Maria glared at Lady Olivia's fool. He'd been missing for days. "Just because you wear that patchwork coat and clown about, doesn't mean you can come and go as you please."

Feste blew a raspberry at her.

"You'd better have a good story," Maria sighed. No one could do anything with Feste. "Here she is now!"

Maria curtseyed low as Lady Olivia came towards them. Tall and slender, she was dressed all in black, in mourning for her father and her brother, her face covered by a veil. Her steward, Malvolio, walked behind her, wearing a gold chain to show his importance.

15

"God bless you, Lady." Feste bowed even lower than Maria, but Lady Olivia barely looked at him; instead she turned to her attendants.

"Take the fool away."

"Do you hear that?" Feste looked around. "Take the lady away."

"I meant you. You're not funny and you're disobedient. Take the fool away."

"You heard her. Take her away."

"I'm not the fool here!"

"You are, my Lady and I'll prove it …"

It was his job to try to cheer her up, and he was also hoping to joke his way back into her good books. He was well on his way to doing just that, and Lady Olivia was smiling despite herself, when Malvolio spoke up.

"I don't know why you put up with this rascal, my Lady."
He glared at Feste. "I've seen funnier clowns in the street."

"Now, Malvolio, don't be so disapproving! Feste is
allowed to tease." Olivia smiled at Feste, who smirked at
Malvolio behind her back.

"My Lady." Maria curtseyed again. "There's a young man
from Duke Orsino waiting to see you."

"Oh, for goodness' sake! Not another! Get rid of him,
Malvolio."

Malvolio came back a few minutes later looking even
more annoyed. "He won't go, my Lady. Whatever I say."

"Oh, all right! I suppose I'd better see him."

Olivia drew her veil closer and Maria threw a veil over her own head. They'd played this trick before. The duke's man wouldn't know which one was mistress and which was maid.

Viola swaggered in, her speech about love learnt and ready. When she saw Lady Olivia and Maria, she stopped and looked from one lady to the other. Who should hear it? She hesitated for a moment, then spoke to the taller of the two.

"I'll speak only to the countess."

It was a lucky guess. Olivia, intrigued by the boy's boldness, sent Maria away.

"What do you want with me?"

"I'll speak only to your face," Viola insisted, trying to see through the veil.

"Oh, very well."

Olivia sighed with impatience and drew back her veil. Viola almost wished she hadn't. She really was beautiful. No wonder Duke Orsino was in love with her. What hope could Viola have? That the lady didn't care for her lord seemed doubly unfair.

"My master loves you …" she began.

"I know that! Get on with it!" Olivia snapped, tired of these messengers from Orsino. Why couldn't he take "no" for an answer? Still, there was something about this one.

"If *I* were to love like Orsino loves you, my Lady, why I – I ..." the boy was saying.

Olivia looked at the boy curiously. "What would you do?"

"I'd camp outside your gate. I'd stay there writing verses and singing love songs, night and day, until you – you took pity on me."

Viola was describing her own love for Duke Orsino. Passionate and sincere, she even shed a tear. Olivia was impressed.

"Go back to your lord," she said. "Tell him I can't love him and to send no more messengers," she paused, "unless *you* come ..." She took a gold coin from her purse. "Here, take this."

"I don't want your money!" Viola refused angrily.
"My master wants your love. I hope you suffer one day
the same way he does! Farewell!"

Olivia stared after the duke's young man in wonder.
He was like no other man she'd met before. A man who
truly knew what it was to love! The icy sadness around
Olivia's heart began to thaw as she realised how quickly
she'd fallen in love. She took a ring from her finger and
called for her steward.

"Malvolio!"

"Yes, my Lady."

"Take this ring. The duke's man left it.
Give it back to him."

"Here, you, boy!" Malvolio shouted after Viola.
"Have this back."

He threw the ring on the ground. Viola bent to pick
it up. She'd left no ring. What could it possibly mean?
There was only one thing it *could* mean. She stood up
slowly, laughing to herself. Lady Olivia thought she was
a man and had fallen in love with her. It couldn't mean
that surely? It would be too ridiculous …

She turned the ring round and looked at it thoughtfully.
She had the proof right here. *I'm in love with Duke Orsino,*
who's in love with Lady Olivia, who's in love with me.
She spun the ring, sending it flashing up into the air, caught
it and put it in her pocket. This was too tangled a knot for
her to untie; she wasn't even going to try!

Chapter 5

"WHAT IS GOING ON?"

Maria stood at the kitchen door, in her nightgown, hands on hips. Gradually, the singing and shouting subsided.

"We were just having a singsong, Maria." Sir Toby put down the saucepan lids he'd been using as cymbals.

"Feste! Get down from that barrel," Maria ordered. "It must be three o'clock in the morning! If my Lady doesn't call Malvolio to throw you out, I don't know what."

"She won't. I'm her uncle! Come on, Maria." Sir Toby began dancing her round the room. "It's only a bit of fun!"

23

He whirled her about to find Malvolio standing in his nightshirt, nightcap on his head, chain of office around his neck.

"Are you all mad? Coming in at this time, making this terrible din? I have to tell you, Sir Toby," said Malvolio, drawing himself up to his full height, bony feet and white ankles showing beneath his long nightshirt, "if you don't behave better, my Lady says you're going."

"Oh, really?" Sir Toby let go of Maria and walked towards the steward. "Who are *you* to tell *me* what to do? Do you think that because *you* don't like fun, *we* should have none?"

"And you, Maria." Malvolio turned on her now. "I'm surprised at you, joining in with this kind of behaviour!"

"But I wasn't! I was trying to stop them!"

"Don't give me excuses! I've got eyes! My Lady will hear of it, don't think she won't. Allowing this kind of thing to go on." He wagged a finger under her nose. "You deserve to be dismissed." Malvolio marched out of the kitchen.

"Oh, go shake your ears!" Maria shouted at his back. "Oooh! That man!" She paced up and down. "I can't stand him. I'll pay him back. I'll make him look a complete fool, you see if I don't!"

"How are you going to do that?" Sir Toby asked.

Sir Andrew and Feste wouldn't mind seeing Malvolio made a fool of, too.

"Yes, tell us, Maria. We want to know!"

"Well, I'll tell you." Maria looked up at their eager faces.
"I'll write a letter, a love letter, and pretend it's from my
lady. I can write just like her. I'll drop it in his way.
He'll pick it up and …"

"He'll think she's in love with him!" Sir Toby slapped
his knee. He could see the joke playing out already.
"Oh, that's good!"

Chapter 6

"Cesario! Come, boy." The duke put his arm round Viola's shoulder. "Walk with me in the garden."

He'd taken to confiding his innermost feelings to the boy who was now his closest companion. He talked about Olivia and how she made him suffer and how women couldn't love in the same way men do.

"Oh, I don't know about that, my Lord."

Viola listened to his sighs, and tried to sympathise, but to say that women didn't feel the pain of love when she was almost dying of love for him, that was too much. To say anything directly would give her away. She had to find some other way to tell him how she felt.

"My father had a daughter," she said. "And *her* love was as strong as any man's." She paused to pick a withered rose. "But she hid her love inside, where it ate away at her."

Viola slowly pulled the petals apart to show
the worm-eaten heart. She wanted to tell him how much
she loved him, but this was as far as she dared go.

"What happened to this girl? Orsino asked. "Did she die
of her love?"

Viola brushed the papery petals from her hands.
"All I can say, sir, is that I'm the only one left of my
father's children."

"Oh, that's sad." The duke shook his head. "Very sad.
Here." He reached into his pocket and brought out
a beautiful tear-shaped pearl. "Take this to Lady Olivia.
Maybe this will convince her of my love."

In Lady Olivia's garden, Maria lay in wait with Sir Toby and Sir Andrew.

"He's coming! Quick. Hide! Not there! Behind the box trees!"

"I'm *so* much better than the others," Malvolio was saying to himself as he walked along, hands behind his back. "My lady *much* prefers me – and ladies *do* marry their servants. I'd be *Count* Malvolio. Sir Toby, I'd say, you must mend your ways…"

"I'm going to hit him!"

"Quiet!" Maria pulled Sir Toby back. "You'll spoil the joke!"

"What's this?" Malvolio stopped to pick up the letter dropped by Maria. "My lady's writing and seal. To … M.O.A.I. Hmm. Those letters are in *my* name. She means me!" He read on. "This is a love letter. To me. What's this she says? *I would like to see you in yellow stockings tied around with garters and smiling all the time.*" Malvolio put the letter next to his heart. "I'll do everything she says."

"Has he gone?"

"Yes." Maria looked out. "Coast's clear."

"Excellent joke, Maria." Sir Andrew hugged her.

"The best! I can't wait to see him." Sir Toby wiped away tears. "Dressed in yellow stockings and grinning from ear to ear."

Chapter 7

"Is your lady in?" Viola asked.

Feste was sitting on the steps of Olivia's house playing his lute.

"Who wants to know?"

"Cesario, the duke's man."

"Duke's *man,* eh?" The look he gave her made her blush. "Aye, she's in. But who you are and what you are, I wouldn't know."

Viola ran up the steps. As soon as Olivia saw her, she ordered everybody else out.

"It's the same every time," Sir Toby grumbled to Sir Andrew. "I don't know what's come over her. She's left off wearing mourning and is throwing herself at the duke's boy …"

When they were alone, Olivia beckoned the young man to sit next to her. She'd dressed with special care and was wearing a beautiful grey silk gown, the same colour as her eyes. She lived for these visits. Every time Cesario came to see her, she fell more and more in love.

"My Lady," Viola started, "my master gives you this …"

"I don't care for your master's gifts!" Olivia set the pearl aside.

"He's giving you his heart, Madam!"

"I don't care for that, either. I don't want to hear any more about him. I'm more interested in *you*." Olivia smiled and moved closer. "I sent you a ring, do you remember? The first time you came here. Surely you could tell what I was feeling? I love you!"

"I'm sorry to disappoint you, Madam." Viola stood up quickly. She had to choose her words carefully. "But no woman has my heart, or ever will have. I must go."

She liked Olivia and didn't want to lie to her, but how could she tell her the truth?

"I'm going home!" Sir Andrew was packing. "Even that boy does better than me!"

"No, Sir Andrew, you can't go now!" Sir Toby could see Sir Andrew's money going, too. "Challenge the duke's boy to a fight. That's the way to win my niece!"

"Good idea!" Sir Andrew stood up. "I'll do just that."

He went off to get ready, leaving Sir Toby helpless with laughter. Sir Andrew was a real coward and the duke's boy didn't look much braver. Their "fight" should be priceless.

Olivia was walking in the garden. She must stop thinking about Cesario. What she needed was someone sad and sensible. Someone like Malvolio. He'd calm her down.

"Maria? Why are you laughing?"

Maria couldn't speak. She shook her head and pointed to Malvolio, walking towards them in yellow stockings, criss-crossed with garters and with a ghastly smile fixed on his face.

"What's the matter with him?" Olivia whispered.

"I've no idea," Maria managed to splutter.

Olivia frowned, he was so unlike his normal self …

"Don't you like my yellow stockings, my Lady?
My garters?"

That smiling was truly terrifying …

"Have him looked after." Olivia turned to her maid.
"I think he's lost his mind."

"Certainly, my Lady."

Maria called for Sir Toby to take Malvolio to the cell.
A night in the darkness would serve him right.

Chapter 8

"I'll have to leave you here." Antonio stopped at the gates of Illyria. "The duke hates me and calls me a pirate."

"I owe you so much, Antonio." Sebastian put a hand on his friend's arm. "You saved me from the sea and looked after me. How can I ever repay you?"

"No need, young master. Look after yourself. Here's my purse, in case you need money. I'll meet you later."

Antonio watched Sebastian walk off alone into the city. It was dangerous for him to be here, but what if Sebastian needed his protection? He had to go after him.

"You men!" The captain of the guard had been watching Antonio. "Follow him. First sign of trouble arrest him!"

"Come with me, young sir." Sir Toby had been lying in wait for Viola. "There's a man. A knight. He wants a fight."

"I'm no fighter!" Viola backed away, hands up. "I'm going in to Lady Olivia."

"Oh, no, you don't!" Sir Toby grabbed her arm.

"What does he want with me? What kind of man is he?"

"The best fighter in all of Illyria. That's the way."

Sir Toby pushed a shaking Viola towards the orchard.

"What's he like?" Sir Andrew whispered to Sir Toby, while Viola fumbled for her sword.

"I've never seen such a swordsman," Sir Toby whispered back. "You'd better watch out!"

Viola and Sir Andrew circled each other, pale and terrified. The last thing either of them wanted was a fight.

"Come on!" Sir Toby pushed them together. They drew their swords, edging closer.

"What's going on here?" Antonio reached for his weapon. He'd decided to look for Sebastian and here he was being threatened, two against one!

"Hey, you!" Suddenly, Duke Orsino's men closed in on him. "You're under arrest!"

"Give me my purse!" Antonio struggled free and put his hand out to Viola.

"What purse? I've never seen you before!"

"Sebastian! I *saved* you and you do this to me!"

The guards dragged Antonio away, leaving Viola to wonder. He called her Sebastian. Could her brother have survived the storm?

"Fancy leaving his friend like that," Sir Toby said, as Viola walked away deep in thought. "Shows you what kind of boy *he* is. A hare's got more courage."

"You're right! I'm going after him," Sir Andrew waved his sword. "Give him a good beating!"

Sir Toby drew his own sword. "Me, too!"

39

Feste had been sent by Olivia to find Cesario. There he was, walking down the street.

"Hey! You! Cesario!" he shouted, but the boy just kept on walking. Feste had to go right up to him and grab his shoulder to make him turn round.

"Cesario? Didn't you hear me? My mistress wants to see you."

"Who's Cesario?" Sebastian frowned. "And who are you?"

"Let me get this straight." Feste looked him up and down. "Your name's not Cesario. My mistress hasn't sent for you. I'm not Feste and this isn't my nose."

"I don't know you." Sebastian stared at the fool. "You don't know me. If I give you money, will you go away?"

"There he is!" Sir Andrew rushed up, sword drawn.
"Take that, Sir!"

Sebastian drew his own sword and struck back.
"And you take that, and that!" He looked round. "Are all
you people mad?"

Sir Toby dragged Sebastian off before he could do
Sir Andrew any more damage and Feste skipped away
to tell Lady Olivia. He wouldn't be in their shoes for
any money.

Sebastian wasn't his sister. He was a man, used to fighting
and quite willing to take on Sir Toby and Sir Andrew.
They circled each other, swords drawn.

41

"They're here!" Feste dragged Olivia by the arm. "Fighting in the street."

"What's all this!" Lady Olivia was furious. "Put up your sword, Toby. How dare you embarrass me like this? Get out of my sight!" She turned to the man she thought was Cesario, "I'm so sorry! Come with me." She gave him her hand. "Let me make it up to you. Please don't say no …"

"Madam, I will."

That was a surprise. Olivia had expected Cesario to say "no", but instead he gripped her hand warmly and let her lead him into her house.

Chapter 9

Sebastian was waiting for Olivia in her garden. He looked down at the pearl she'd given him. He still couldn't believe that this was happening. Was he dreaming? They'd only met that morning but it was as if she'd known him for a long time …

"There you are!" Olivia took Sebastian's hand. "If we're meant for each other, we should go to the church and swear our love." Olivia was taking no chances. She'd brought a priest with her. Cesario seemed to have undergone a complete change of heart and she didn't want him changing his mind now. "What do you say?"

She looked at Sebastian, her grey eyes imploring.
She really was very beautiful and for reasons he couldn't
quite understand obviously adored him. She was rich and
commanded a large household. He made his mind up
quickly. He could do far worse …

"I'll go with you, Madam, and swear to always be true."

There was no time to waste! Olivia waved the priest on.
"Lead the way, good father!"

"I'm getting nowhere with this." Duke Orsino strode
out of his palace. "I'm going to see her myself.
You men come with me. And you, Cesario."

Viola and two attendants followed quickly.
Just before they got to Lady Olivia's house,
they came face to face with two
guards marching Antonio
between them.

"Duke Orsino," said Antonio, shaking off his captors. "I know we're enemies but I risked coming to Illyria to protect this boy. Now he pretends he doesn't know me. He even refused to return my purse."

"Cesario?" The Duke frowned. "When did he come here?"

"Why, just this morning …"

"How can that be?" Orsino's frown deepened. "He's been with me for weeks now."

This was a mystery, but Orsino had no time to puzzle it out. Lady Olivia was leaving her house, accompanied by her maid and a priest.

"Orsino? What are you doing here? Cesario? My love? Why are you with him?"

Cesario? My love? Orsino looked from Lady Olivia to his servant and back again. How could it be? She loved another. Not only that but his own man, who'd obviously been courting her on his own account. Won her, too, by the look of it.

Orsino grabbed Viola by her collar. "You'll never have him! Here boy, come with me."

Viola didn't even struggle. She loved Orsino so much she would gladly go with him anywhere.

How could anyone be so two-faced? Olivia couldn't believe her eyes.

"You can't go." Olivia pulled Viola back towards her. "The priest is a witness. We're engaged to be married."

"Married!"

Viola was as shocked as Orsino. "Me? No! No!"

"That's him." The priest nodded. "Definitely."

"Why, you lying little cub!" Orsino pushed Viola away. "Go to her then. I never want to see you again!"

"But my Lord!"

Suddenly, Sir Andrew
stumbled towards them,
holding a handkerchief to
his head. "A doctor!
And for Sir Toby."

"More fighting!
Who's done this to you,
Sir Andrew?" Olivia put
out a hand to help him.

"The duke's man,
Cesario." Sir Andrew
jumped back. "That's
him! Don't hit me again."

"Why do you speak to
me?" Viola stared. "I never
hurt you!"

"What's this look like?" Sir Andrew pointed to
a graze on his cheek. "And look at Sir Toby."

Sir Toby appeared holding a handkerchief to *his* head.

"Take them away, Maria." Olivia turned to her maid.
"Have their wounds seen to."

Sir Andrew and Sir Toby hurried off. They could see
Sebastian striding towards them.

"Madam, I'm sorry if I hurt your kinsman," he said as he put up his sword. "I was coming through the garden when they set upon me for a *second* time! I … What's the matter?"

No one was listening. They were too busy looking from Sebastian to Cesario, from brother to sister.

Duke Orsino found his voice first. "Same face, same clothes," he said in wonder, "but two different people."

"Are you Sebastian?" Antonio asked.

"Of course I am!"

"Have you split yourself in half? An apple cut in two is not more alike."

Then Sebastian saw Viola.

"I never had a brother …" Sebastian stared at her. "I had a sister but she was drowned." He reached towards her. "Where are you from? Who are your parents?"

"I'm from Messalina," Viola answered, putting her hand up to his. "Sebastian was my father. I had a brother also named Sebastian, but he was drowned …"

"And I had a sister … If you were a woman, I'd say, welcome back, drowned Viola!"

"But I *am* Viola!"

Brother and sister held each other tightly, scarcely able to believe that the other was still alive.

Orsino watched in wonder. So much that he hadn't understood suddenly made sense. Knowing she was a girl changed everything.

"Viola …" He tried out the new name.

"Yes, my Lord." Viola turned to him.

"You told me many times you'd never love a woman." He didn't quite know how put this. "Could that mean, does that mean, that you love *me*?"

"Oh, yes!"

"In that case, Viola …" Orsino took her hand. "Will you marry me?"

"There's nothing I want more in the world!" She looked down at her doublet and hose. "Once I've changed into women's clothes."

"My Lord, if it please you," Olivia smiled at Orsino, happy for him to wed another. "We can all be married in my house."

"That's a very good idea." Orsino kissed Viola's hand and smiled. "I can't wait for you to be my wife."

Olivia took her other hand. "You'll be my sister …"

"Madam, you've done me wrong!"

"Malvolio?" Olivia had forgotten all about him.

"Look at this!" He thrust a letter into her hand.

"This is Maria's writing." She looked down at the paper. "You were tricked, Malvolio. I'm sorry." She smiled at him. "I'll make it up to you."

"Don't bother!" Malvolio turned his back on them.
He stomped off, muttering, "I'll be revenged upon
the whole pack of you."

"Go after him!" Orsino ordered one of his men. "I don't
want anyone or anything to spoil this happy, golden time."

The couples joined hands and the priest led the way into
Olivia's house where they were to be married.

Feste, left alone, picked up his lute and began to pick out
a tune. Weddings were a time for laughter and song.

Playing a part

Boy

"I'll disguise myself
as a boy."

Lover

"Don't you like my yellow
stockings, my Lady?"

Fool

"Duke's man, eh?"

Fighter

Pale and terrified.

Playing for real

Girl

Knowing she was a girl
changed everything.

Lover

"Swear our love."

Fool

"We were just having
a singsong!"

Fighter

He was a man used
to fighting.

Ideas for reading

Written by Clare Dowdall, PhD
Lecturer and Primary Literacy Consultant

Reading objectives:

- check that the book makes sense to them, discussing their understanding and exploring the meaning of words in context
- ask questions to improve their understanding
- predict what might happen from details stated and implied

Spoken language objectives:

- participate in discussions, presentations, performances, role play, improvisations and debates

Curriculum links: PSHE – relationships

Resources: ICT for research, art materials for drawing

Build a context for reading

- Explain that *Twelfth Night* is a famous comedy play by William Shakespeare.
- Ask children to look at the front cover and describe what they can see happening. What do they think the characters are doing?
- Read the blurb to the children. Check that they understand the terms used, e.g. "hilarity" and "mistaken identities".

Understand and apply reading strategies

- Turn to the cast of characters and help children to read the names. Explain that Viola and Sebastian are twins.
- Ask children to read silently to p8. Lead a discussion about the character of Viola. Ask children to suggest adjectives to describe her at the beginning of this story.